This Is the Rope

A STORY FROM THE GREAT MIGRATION

JACQUELINE WOODSON

illustrated by JAMES RANSOME

PUFFIN BOOKS

AUTHOR'S NOTE: My mother arrived in New York City by bus in 1968. There she joined her sister, Caroline, who had left South Carolina four years earlier. In 1969, my uncle Robert joined his older sisters in the small apartment they rented in the Brownsville section of Brooklyn. In late 1970, after the death of my grandfather, my grandmother joined her children up north. My mother had by then moved to a larger place in the Bushwick section of Brooklyn. This area of Brooklyn, I would later learn, was settled by a group of Dutchmen including Jan Francisco, who had once been enslaved but worked to buy his freedom. For many years my mother would rent this apartment in Bushwick. Eventually, she would own the building. Like many African Americans migrating north during this period, my mother's dream was to one day own her own home.

Between 1968 and 1970, my sister, brothers and I traveled back and forth between South Carolina and New York. It wouldn't be until many years later that I learned we were part of a long history: From the early 1900s until the mid 1970s, more than 6 million African Americans moved from the rural South to northern cities. The cities included Chicago, Los Angeles, and of course, my own beloved New York City. We came for better jobs, better treatment, better education and better lives. This movement of Blacks from the South to the North would become known as the Great Migration.

And while my mother and grandmother held fast their memories of the South (their southern accents remained with them both until their passing), they had dreams for us that only the freedom of the North could make true.

This Is the Rope is a work of fiction. The rope we brought to this "new country" was Hope.

It remains with us.

—J.W.

PUFFIN BOOKS An imprint of Penguin Random House LLC 375 Hudson Street New York, New York 10014

First published in the United States of America by Nancy Paulsen Books, an imprint of Penguin Young Readers Group, 2013. Published by Puffin Books, an imprint of Penguin Random House LLC, 2017.

Text copyright © 2013 by Jacqueline Woodson. Illustrations copyright © 2013 by James Ransome.

Design by Ryan Thomann. The illustrations were done in oil on paper.
Endpaper pattern copyright © 2013 by Diane Labombarbe.

CIP DATA IS AVAILABLE UPON REQUEST.
ISBN 978-0-399-23986-1 (HC)
Puffin Books ISBN 9780425288948

Manufactured in China

10 9 8 7 6 5 4 3 2 1

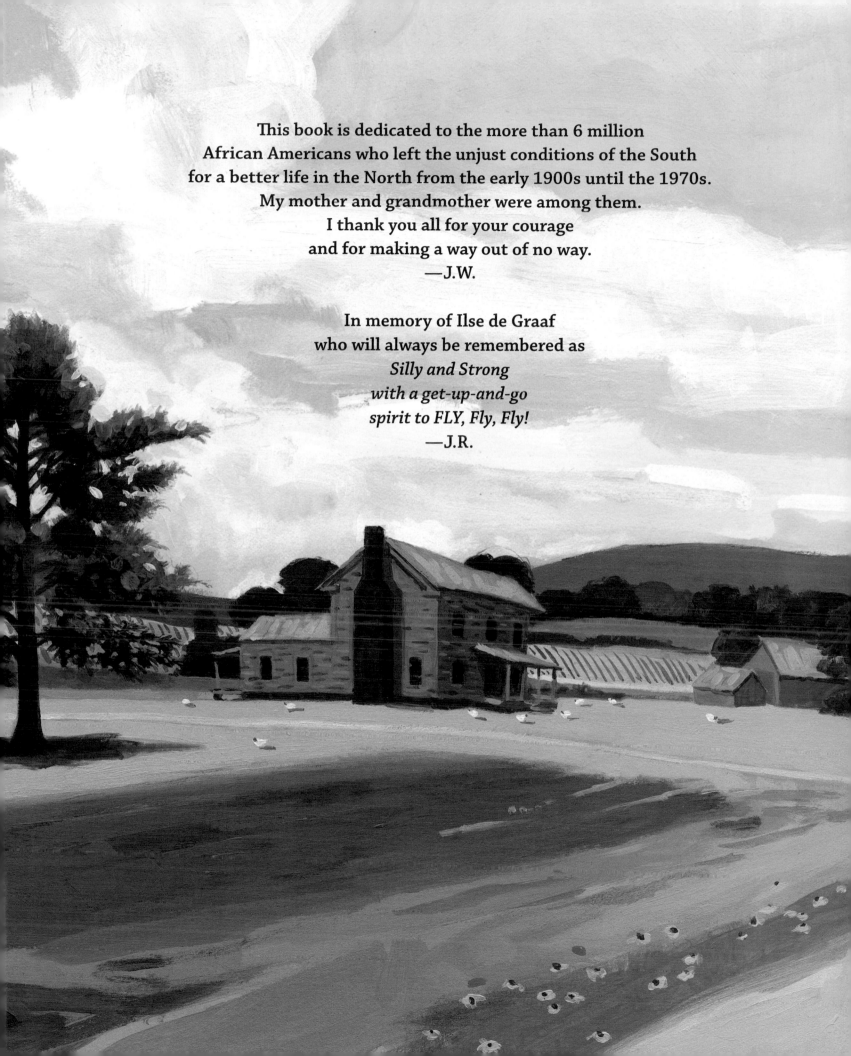

This book is dedicated to the more than 6 million
African Americans who left the unjust conditions of the South
for a better life in the North from the early 1900s until the 1970s.
My mother and grandmother were among them.
I thank you all for your courage
and for making a way out of no way.
—J.W.

In memory of Ilse de Graaf
who will always be remembered as
Silly and Strong
with a get-up-and-go
spirit to FLY, Fly, Fly!
—J.R.

This is the rope my grandmother found
beneath an old tree
a long time ago
back home in South Carolina.

This is the rope my grandmother skipped
under the shade of a sweet-smelling pine.

This is the rope my grandfather used
to tie the few things they owned
to the top of a car that drove my grandmother,

who was a mother now,
from South Carolina all the long way to a place called
New York City.

This is the rope my grandmother held tight to
as my grandfather drove
real slow past the people and big city buildings
that seemed to go on and on . . .

This is the rope my grandmother used
to dry the sweet-smelling flowers
she grew in small window boxes
reminding her of the flowers *back home.*
Where the land, she said, *went on and on . . .*

This is the rope my grandfather strung
so that my mama's diapers could
blow dry in the hot city breeze.

And this is the rope my mama tied
around a small duckie's neck,
then pulled it along, singing
quack, quack, quack.

This is the rope my mama held out to the girls on the block,
her new Brooklyn block, a home of their own
that they *finally* owned.

Mama asked shyly,
Anybody want to play?

This is the rope my mama first tripped on
as she sang with her friends,

"Miss Lucy had a baby,

she named

This is the rope Mama's brothers took from her room for some crazy game that little boys play.

This is the rope my mama found again,
ten years later, when my grandfather said,
We need a bit of rope to tie these things down
inside this here car, like that rope
we used to have from back home.
Then he drove with my mama,
off to a college far away from the city,
while up at the window, my grandmother waved.

This is the rope my mama placed
on the piano around family photos
and me just a baby and then a bit bigger
already reaching for it.

This is the rope my daddy used
when he showed me the way
to tie a sailor's knot—
Two times around and pull it real tight.
You want whatever you make or do
in your life, my daddy said, *to last . . .*

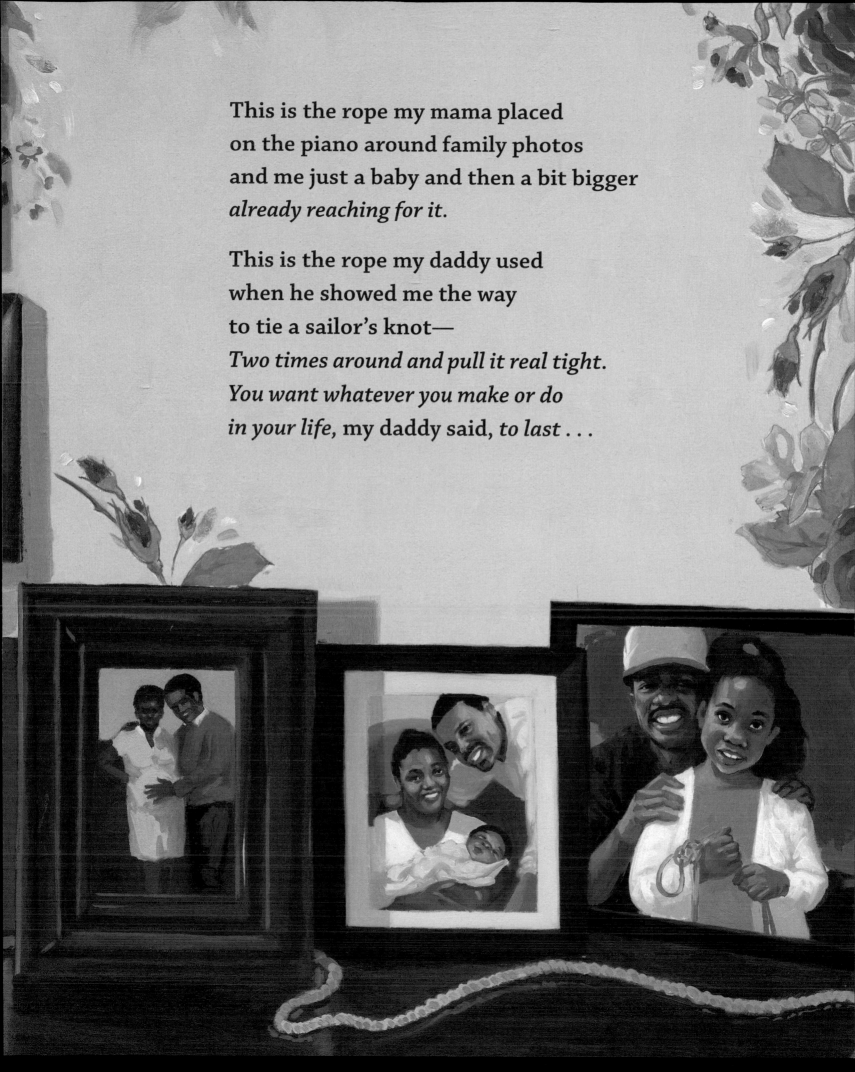

This is the rope my mama turned
as she waved to my daddy
and taught me to sing
the Miss Lucy song out on our sidewalk
right here in Brooklyn,
just last Friday night.

This is the rope that held up the sign saying
We Are All Family
at our picnic reunion in the big park
up the street from our home.

This is the rope, threadbare and graying,
that I traded with Grandma for a brand-new one.
Then I jumped a new jump:
B, my name is Beatrice, I come from Brooklyn . . .

As my family smiled proudly and the sun began setting,
as Grandma held on to her rope from *back home* . . .

. . . and her long-ago memory of sweet-smelling pine.